206

WHERE PEOPLE LIVE

ANGELA ROYSTON

RAINTREE
STECK-VAUGHN
PUBLISHERS
The Steck-Vaughn Company

Austin, Texas

Published by Raintree Steck-Vaughn Publishers,
an imprint of Steck-Vaughn Company

Library of Congress Cataloging-in-Publication Data
Royston, Angela.
Where people live / Angela Royston.
     p.   cm.—(Geography starts here)
     Includes bibliographical references and index.
     Summary: Explores the reasons why people live
     in various geographical regions and how they
     survive, discussing towns, cities, and dwellings
     in mountains or next to water.
     ISBN 0-8172-5116-2
     1. Human geography—Juvenile literature.
     2. Dwellings—Juvenile literature.
     [1. Dwellings. 2. Human geography.]
     I. Title. II. Series.
     GF48.R69 1998
     304.2—dc21   97-29909

Printed in Italy. Bound in the United States.
1 2 3 4 5 6 7 8 9 0 03 02 01 00 99

Picture Acknowledgments
Pages 2: James Davis Travel Photography. 5: James Davis Travel Photography.
6-7: Zefa/Stockmarket/D. C. Johnson. 7: Wayland Picture Library. 8: Eye Ubiquitous/Hugh Rooney.
9: James Davis Travel Photography. 10: Zefa Photo Library. 11: Wayland Picture Library.
12: Eye Ubiquitous/L. Fordyce. 13: Zefa Photo Library. 14: Zefa/Orion Press. 15: Eye Ubiquitous/M.
Feeney. 16: Eye Ubiquitous/David Cumming. 17: Aerofilms/Wayland. 18: Wayland Picture Library.
19: Zefa Photo Library. 20: Eye Ubiquitous/Adina Tovy Amsel. 21: James Davis Travel Photography.
22: FLPA/L. Lee Rue. 23: Impact Photos/Christopher Bluntzer. 24: DAS/David Simson. 25: James
Davis Travel Photography. 26: Wayland Picture Library/Chris Fairclough. 27: Wayland Picture
Library. 28: Zefa Photo Library. 29: James Davis Travel Photography. 31: Wayland Picture Library.

The title page shows a view of the city of Rio de Janeiro, Brazil.

CONTENTS

ALL OVER THE WORLD

There are nearly 6 billion people living on the earth. Each of us needs somewhere to rest and sleep. You may live in the countryside, or you may live in a town or city.

Most people live in houses or apartments. Some live in tents or trailers and some live on boats. Some people are nomads. They move from place to place.

This map shows the world's major cities.

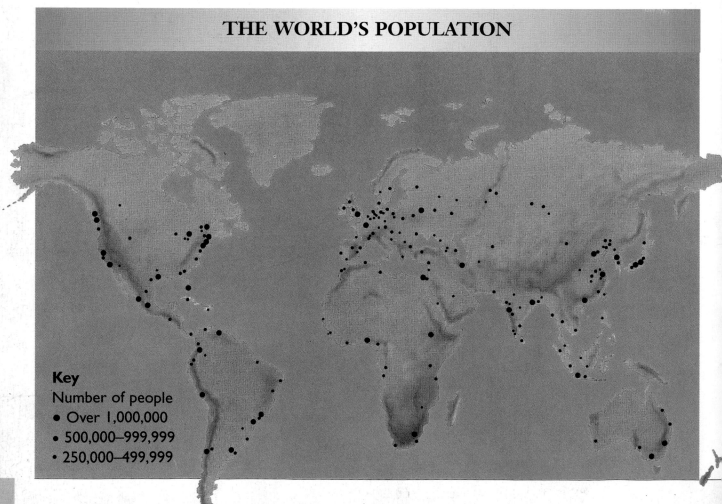

THE WORLD'S POPULATION

Key
Number of people
- Over 1,000,000
- 500,000–999,999
- 250,000–499,999

Houses overlook canals in Venice, Italy. Boats called gondolas carry people around the city.

5

SETTLEMENTS

A settlement is a place where people live. There are many different kinds of settlements, from small villages to big cities.

No matter where they live, people need food, water, and shelter. They also need fuel for cooking, heat, and light.

Large, 19th-century houses line streets in San Francisco.

Most people depend on jobs on farms, in factories, and in offices. They earn money to buy things they need. In some places people grow most of their own food.

A mailman delivers mail by camel to a small settlement in India.

Ideal Places

In the past, people built settlements where there was plenty of water, food, and fuel. They often chose places by the sea or on a river because there they could trade with people from other places.

Trade is still very important. Factories are built close to fast roads and ports so that goods can be transported quickly. Factories also provide jobs, attracting many people to move to these areas.

Tall buildings surround the harbor at Monte Carlo in Monaco.

A crowded street market in London, England. Here, people can buy food, clothes, and household goods.

These houses are in the Highland region of Scotland. In much of Scotland there are only a few houses in a huge area of countryside.

All around the world, billions of people live in small villages and towns. Villages look different in each region of the world. Builders use local materials—stone, brick, wood, or mud—and design the houses to suit the weather conditions of the region.

In small villages most people know each other. They meet in the local stores and their children go to the same schools.

Boats carry freight to and from this coastal town in Portugal.

Towns

Villages often grow into towns as industry develops or because the weekly markets attract local farmers. Some in the mountains or by the sea become vacation resorts.

Some towns grow into cities. People move there looking for work, and more houses are built. Gradually, the city spreads and is linked with surrounding villages. In some cities the poorest people build their own homes in makeshift areas called shantytowns.

The people living in these shelters in Dacca, Bangladesh, have just arrived from the countryside.

This hilltop monastery overlooks a small town in Spain. Most of the houses were built around it during the Middle Ages.

Washing hangs out the windows of this tall apartment building in Singapore.

Cities

Cities are settlements where there are many people and buildings. The tallest buildings are called skyscrapers. Many people can live and work on a small area of land.

Homes and factories are usually built away from the city center, in suburbs. Most suburbs have their own stores, schools, and parks.

Skyscraper offices and apartments tower over Tokyo, Japan.

Capital Cities

Each country's government is located in its capital city. The capital is not always the country's largest city, but it is usually where the main government offices are.

Traffic fills the streets in Bangkok, the capital of Thailand.

The capital city is usually a hub for transportation and communication. Airports connect the capital with other cities or countries.

This aerial view of London, the capital of England, shows parkland, houses, factories, docks, and the Thames River.

17

ON THE MOVE

The most convenient way to get from one place to another is by car, but too many cars jam the streets. Most cities have several different kinds of transportation to help people move about easily.

Many people cycle to and from work in the rush-hour in Beijing, the capital of China.

SLOW OR FAST?

Which is the fastest means of transport? On a regular long journey, record the time it takes when you travel by car, bus, bicycle, and on foot. Which is the fastest way? Traffic jams often make car journeys the slowest by far.

Buses or trolleys may each each carry as many as 100 people. Smaller buses and taxis take people short distances. Trains speed people into and out of city centers. Many cities have trains that run under the ground.

This photo of New York City shows people on the move by car, taxi, and bicycle.

These people are having fun roller skating in Central Park, New York City.

20

OPEN SPACES

Most cities have parks and gardens, where people can get away from the noise of the traffic. Here they run, play football and other sports, or just relax.

There are many ways to enjoy yourself in a city. You can see famous buildings or visit museums and theaters. If you want to buy a souvenir, you can choose from many different kinds.

People sit and relax outside cafés along a canal in Amsterdam, the Netherlands.

UNUSUAL HOMES

Some people live far away from anyone else.
In Australia and Argentina, cattle ranches
and sheep farms are so big that some farmers
use small planes to get to the nearest town.

In most countries farms are much smaller.
In India and Africa, many people grow just
enough food for themselves with a little left
over to sell at a local market.

A farmer herds some
cattle at a ranch in the
countryside in Canada.

A family in front of its mud and straw house in a tiny village in Kenya, Africa.

In the Mountains

High in the mountains the air is thin and cold. Life is very hard there. Yet thousands of people live in mountain villages.

Many mountain people herd animals and work for tourists and climbers. Some of these people have two homes. In spring and summer they move higher up the mountain where their animals can feed on fresh grass.

HIGH LIFE

On the map on page 4, how many cities can you find on mountains (the light-brown areas)? Living on high mountains is very difficult. But land near mountains gets lots of rain and has many rivers. On the map, are there many cities next to mountains?

People board a bus in the Andes Mountains in Ecuador, South America.

24

This hillside chalet is near the Matterhorn mountain in Switzerland.

Hong Kong is overcrowded. There is no room to build new houses. Many people live on boats called junks.

Living Next to Water

People have always liked to live near water. The sea and rivers provide fish. Rivers also give a good supply of fresh water. It is easier to travel by boat than over the land.

Groups of houses and farmland stretch along the banks of the Danube River in Austria.

Today some of these old settlements have grown into busy ports and towns, but there are still many fishing villages on the coast.

NEW TOWNS AND CITIES

Most cities have grown from villages and towns. But a few cities have been built in the middle of the countryside. New cities are planned to avoid the problems of the old cities, such as overcrowding.

This modern housing area is in Texas. Each house has its own yard and driveway. Many houses have swimming pools.

With no traffic, people can shop peacefully and safely in this shopping mall in Atlanta, Georgia.

Most cities and towns, however, have developed over a long period of time. Their streets and buildings may be different sizes and styles, and they may appear strange. But they have excitement and energy.

FACTS AND FIGURES

Largest country
The Russian Federation is the largest country in the world. It is nearly twice as large as Canada, the second largest country. The Russian Federation stretches from Europe to the Pacific and takes eight days to cross by train.

Smallest country
Vatican City is an independent country in the middle of Rome in Italy. It is no bigger than a city park and less than 1,000 people live there.

Highest population
More than 1,200,000,000 people live in China, but India is catching up fast.

Emptiest country
For every person in Western Sahara there is more than a quarter square mile (sq. km) of land. This is not surprising because Western Sahara is almost entirely desert.

Most crowded country
Over half a million people live in the tiny country of Macao. It has about 30,000 people in each quarter square mile (sq. km).

Highest city
Lhasa is nearly 13,000 ft. (4,000 m) above the level of the sea. Lhasa is the main city of Tibet, a mountainous region between China and India. Tibet is sometimes called the "roof of the world." Tibet used to be an independent country until it was conquered by China.

Highest capital city
La Paz is in the Andes Mountains in South America. It is the capital of Bolivia and is almost as high as Lhasa.

City with most people
Tokyo, the capital city of Japan, has grown so big it has joined up with nearby Yokohama to form one huge city with about 25 million people. Mexico City and São Paulo are growing fast.

Oldest city
There has been a city at Jericho near Jerusalem in Israel for about 10,000 years.

Coldest town
The coldest town is Oymyakon in Siberia in eastern Russia. The temperature there has fallen to -94° F (-70° C).

Tallest skyscrapers
Two tower blocks in Kuala Lumpur in Malaysia are 1,476 ft. (450 m) high.

Tent homes
Nomads live in deserts. They wander across the land with their animals looking for plants to graze. They carry their tent homes with them.

Floating homes
Some people live in boats rather than houses. In cities built along rivers old barges are homes to many people.

Further Reading

Dorros, Arthur. *This is My House*. New York: Scholastic Hardcover, 1992.

Jackson, Mike. *Homes Around the World*. Austin, TX: Raintree Steck-Vaughn, 1995.

James, Alan. *Homes in Cold Places* (Houses and Homes). Minneapolis, MN: Lerner Group, 1989.

——. *Homes in Hot Places* (Houses and Homes). Minneapolis, MN: Lerner Group, 1989.

——. *Homes on Water* (Houses and Homes). Minneapolis, MN: Lerner Group, 1989.

Oxlade, Chris. *Houses and Homes* (Technology Craft Topics). Danbury, CT: Franklin Watts, 1994.

GLOSSARY

Billion A thousand million, that is 1,000,000,000.

Climate The usual kind of weather in a region.

Country An area of land that has its own government. Most people in a country speak the same language.

Fuel Something, such as wood, coal or gas, which is burned to give heat or light.

Government The group of people who run a country. The government decides how much money will be spent on roads, schools, hospitals, the army, and so on.

Local Not far from home.

Polar lands Very cold lands around the North and South poles where the ground is always covered by ice.

Ranches The name for certain types of farms in the United States, Australia, South America, and Africa.

Restaurant A place where people can buy and eat a meal that has been cooked for them.

Suburbs The outer parts of a town or city, built around its central area.

Trade Buying and selling goods.

Traffic All the vehicles, such as cars, trucks, buses, and vans, that move along a road.

A busy street scene in Calcutta, India

INDEX